BILLIONAIRE'S SEXY RANGER

GAY ROMANCE

GAY BILLIONAIRES
BOOK ONE

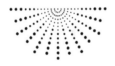

DILLON HART

CHAPTER ONE

JETT

"We'll be coming up to the ranger station in a few minutes," the helicopter pilot says. "Prepare for landing."

His voice crackles in the earphones of my headset, only just about audible over the noise of the helicopter's rotor blades.

I take my eyes off of the open folder in my lap I've been engrossed in for most of the journey, and look out of the small window next to my seat.

What I see almost takes my breath away. Vast, rolling plains as far as the eye can see. Wildflower meadows, streams and outcrops of trees, and scrub dot the land-scape. There's an occasional dirt track or path, looking just as though they have been made from herds of mustang or wild cattle than by human activity.

"Wow. That sure is something," I say absently, forgetting the open mic on my headset.

There's a grunt of assent in response, and I glance at my four-strong entourage in turn. Three of my senior board members, and our aide.

All four are a pain in my ass. Even if it is their job to be.

"Sure is, boss," Mike Lincoln, my company's Director of Operations, responds. "I haven't seen a single soul since that last farmstead we flew over an hour ago."

Mike's the only guy that actually volunteered for the trip, and is heavily involved in the company's charitable foundations. One of the few who actually cares.

There's a snort from my Chief Financial Officer, Linda Jones, and I glance over at her, eyebrows raised.

"You know what I see?" she says with a half smile as she peers out of the window. "I see...a vast cattle ranch, stretching as far as the eye can see. With an on-site slaughterhouse or two, and a distribution center for delivering the fresh meat. I see oil and natural gas prospecting..."

I bark a harsh laugh.

"You see dollar signs," I say drily. "Don't say anything like that in front of the tree hugger. She won't like it. Oh, and she's probably got a rifle or two."

"He."

I look over at my aide and PA, Lyle. I frown, and he smiles back.

"*He* won't like it. Casey, the park ranger. I actually googled this guy, and Casey just happens to be a man," he adds with sarcasm.

I shrug and turn my eyes back to the natural beauty of the surrounding countryside.

"I *may* have skim read the brief," I mutter.

Still, I know I'd memorized the core aims of the project and what the ranger is here to do, so I don't look like a disinterested sugar daddy, in it just for the positive PR.

And I've always got the caring ex-veterinarian card to play. The carefully hidden ace up my sleeve.

"Brace for landing," the pilot's voice barks into my headset. "Weather conditions are optimal. Should be nice and smooth."

The helicopter pivots as it descends, and a large wooden cabin comes into view through the window. The cabin has a grass roof and a low profile, and if it wasn't for the solar panels and radio antenna, it would seem right at place in its wild surroundings.

A figure emerges from the cabin as the helicopter lands with a gentle bump, and the rotor blades whirl to a slow stop.

The ranger is wearing worn out leather cowboy boots, a pair of old blue jeans, and a loose, checkered lumberjack shirt. His unkempt and long blonde hair is whipped up, as he strides towards the helicopter. He stops a short distance away, arms crossed over his chest as he waits.

I'm momentarily frozen at the sight of him. Despite his plain, almost ragged clothes, he's an incredibly beautiful man, even with that ugly sunburn. He has a serious, almost impatient expression on his strong features. His tousled blond hair frames his prominent cheekbones, making him look like some sort of woodland god, resplendent in his natural setting.

I tear my eyes away from him, and unconsciously smooth out my shirt and suit jacket as I rise from my seat to a crouch, and swing open the door of the helicopter. The pilot is there, and offers me a supportive arm, but I wave him away and leap from the door to land gracefully on my expensive leather shoes.

I turn back to the helicopter and catch the rucksack that's thrown down to me, containing a change of clothes. I've been hoping for a more "hands-on" tour; something I knew my associates would definitely not be keen on. But still, I'm the boss.

And now that I've seen my would-be tour guide, I'm even more keen for something a little more… intimate.

I turn back to our waiting host, and make my way over to him. I put on my warmest, most charming smile as I approach, hand held out on greeting. Something flashes in his eyes as they meet mine, and his expression brightens for a moment. Then, suddenly, he's back to his guarded, impatient facade.

"You must be Casey," I say, maintaining my warm smile. "I'm Jett. Jett Baxter."

He frowns a little and purses his surprisingly full lips into a thoughtful pout as he studies me. My heart races, and I try to hide the growing desire I feel coursing through me.

After a moment he takes my hand in a quick grasp. His skin is rough and warm, and his handshake is almost aggressively strong.

"I'm the ranger," he replies. "Casey Taylor. So are you the guy in charge?"

I glance over my shoulder at the figures emerging from the helicopter.

"That's me," I say. "Though these guys would have me believe otherwise!"

A smile flashes over his face, disappearing just as quickly as it had come.

"Listen, Jett," he says, voice low and serious. "I'm gonna be frank with you. I know this is a PR stunt, and while I appreciate the attention, I'm here to do a job. I also know that without your funding I wouldn't have this job, but I'm out here alone, and I'm busy as hell."

He gestures for me to follow him towards the lodge.

"Plus," he continues, "there's a series of storms forecast, with a chance of hurricane force winds and flash flooding. Next day or so, maybe sooner. I need to get the cabin prepared, and make sure my most urgent errands around the reserve are done before the storms hit."

I look over at the comfortable looking wooden lodge. An old, yet robust truck is parked to one side. Two horses are tethered in a nearby stable, snouts buried into feedbags, munching away contentedly.

"Well, I'm sorry for the interruption," I say, a little annoyed at him for basically telling me I'm wasting his time. "But we're keen to see the work our considerable funding is doing, as I hope you'll understand. It's not just about the PR. I... *we* care about what's going on here, and the work you're doing."

I immediately feel bad at my response, but I don't want Casey to assume I'm some rich asshole who's doing this just to look good. I decide to try and change the subject, for a moment at least.

"You're out here all alone?" I ask. "How do you find it? Doesn't it get lonely at all?"

He shrugs.

"I knew what I was in for when I took the job. Most of the time I'm too busy to get lonely. Plus I enjoy the work, and the peace and solitude."

He whistles a shrill, high-pitched whistle, and I hear the frantic scrabbling of claws on wood coming from the cabin's open door. A moment later a small, scraggy dog appears in a flash, and hurtles towards Casey.

He drops to his knees and greets the dog as it approaches. I realize as it launches itself into his lap, tail wagging madly, that it's three legged. Not that that seems to have slowed it down.

"And I've got my ball of fluff to keep me company," he says fondly. "I rescued him when he was a puppy, abandoned after being hit by a car in the city."

I settle down into a crouch and hold out a hand in greeting. The dog approaches to sniff my hand, and then rolls onto his back in subservient greeting. Casey laughs as he watches me scratch the dog, a deep, warm sound that sends tingles of pleasure through me.

"What's his name?" I ask.

I look over at Casey. He's leaning forward, hands on his big, strong looking quads. His loose flannel shirt suddenly becomes tight in all the right places. I glance at his narrow hips, and slim, athletic waist. A gust of wind billows the front of his shirt, and I catch a glimpse of a broad, well-muscled chest, sprinkled with a smattering of golden chest hair and hidden beneath a white undershirt.

His expression is soft as he studies me and the dog. He obviously cares deeply for the scraggy, yet strangely adorable animal.

"Ted," he says. "He likes you. He's probably just glad to have the new company."

I hear the sound of voices approaching, and I rise to my feet. I turn to see my entourage approaching, serious and businesslike in the tone of voice and expressions, each one trying their best to look as impatient and disinterested as possible.

I sigh, suddenly wishing I was here alone.

"Well, here we go," I say sadly. "Back to business."

Casey rises to his feet to stand next to me, crossing his arms over his chest once again, and adopting an impatient pose.

A feeling comes over me as my team approaches, and I sense a sudden tension in the air. I suddenly have the gut feeling that there's going to be a clash of strong personalities at some point, and I clench my teeth in anticipation.

CHAPTER TWO

CASEY

Jett is different to what I expected, but I still can't help but feel like this whole thing is both an intrusion, and a complete waste of my time. Surely they could have visited headquarters, and been given a polished presentation by one of the suits who'd be keen on kissing asses? Why did I have to get encumbered with this?

In the few months I've been working on the reserve, I've gotten used to the solitude, and the ranger cabin is my sanctuary. I feel strangely violated by the presence of these suit clad, briefcase clutching people.

"So," Lyle, Jett's aide and PA says, after brief introductions. "Jett and his executive team are keen to see the work that's being done with the company's charitable contributions. I chose the mustang reserve as an ideal place to visit, one because it's one of our most ambitious projects to date, and two, because it's relatively close to our next *engagement*."

He puts emphasis on the word engagement, and glares at Jett.

Jett sighs, exasperated.

"You mean the Smithson deal? I told you I don't need to be there for that. I can't hold our sales team's hands every time they get a difficult client, Lyle," he replies, his tone icy.

Lyle spreads his arms in an attempt to placate his boss.

"I think it would be best if you were here for this one. That's why I prepared the file for you. I hope you've studied it," Lyle says, as if the argument has already been decided in his favor, merely by him assuming that's the case.

I glare at the two in turn. Jett opens his mouth to continue the argument.

I raise my hands in irritation.

"Listen, guys!" I say. "I'm behind enough as it is, and with the storms coming in, I'd appreciate it if we could hurry this along."

The CFO, whose name I've already forgotten, glances at me, eyes wide. Then she glares at her aide.

"Storms? You didn't say anything about storms, Lyle. And we're here in a damned helicopter, of all things. Let's get this over with quickly, and get to the city, shall we. I'd take a five-star hotel over this old cabin any day."

She looks at me sheepishly.

"No offense," she adds.

I shrug.

"None taken. Now, I've got two horses, and the old truck. Obviously neither of those options is going to carry all of us together. But, luckily, there's a place I can take you to that's around twenty minutes walk, where we should be able to get a glimpse of a mustang herd that's been grazing in a pasture we prepared for them. I was hoping they'd stop so we can monitor them more closely, and as luck would have it…"

I start to walk as I talk, heading towards the gate at the entrance to the field the cabin is in. Lyle steps in front of me, stopping me in my tracks, a finger raised.

"Well, uh, Casey?" he says, his voice rising in a patronising manner. "We've got the helicopter? I was thinking we could take a quick tour, maybe for an hour or two, see the herds, the projects you're working on, drop you back and then we'd be on our way."

I frown at him, and continue walking. He steps to one side at the last moment.

"No," I reply flatly. "I don't want us scaring the herds. They're free to roam as they please, but we're trying to encourage herds, through various initiatives and projects, to stick to a specified area. It makes identifying and monitoring them much easier, and I don't want them to bolt, ruining the slow progress we've made so far."

I hear a sigh from Lyle.

Probably just doesn't want to scuff those expensive shoes, or crease his shirt before his oh-so important meeting.

"But we-"

"Lyle, that's enough!" Jett says sternly. "Casey's in charge here. He says no helicopter, that means no helicopter."

I feel a strange glow of satisfaction at Jett's support, but I push it down. I can't help but think he's just trying to convince me he's not an arrogant, impatient suit like his entourage. And, I know, he's showing me who's *really* in charge.

"Well, I'm staying here," comes a female voice from behind me. "I'm not walking for twenty minutes in these heels. I'm afraid it's helicopter or nothing."

I swivel on my heel, feeling irritation rise within me. I've already wasted enough of my time, and these supposed grown men and woman arguing like children are starting to piss me off.

"Same here," adds the CFO. "We'll stay and prepare for the Smithson presentation. You lot go ahead."

Lyle stands between those two, and me, Jett, and the DOO, the only person other than Jett who hasn't had a word of complaint so far.

"So you're telling me you've come all this way to look at a log cabin, two domesticated horses and an old truck?" Lyle asks the pair.

He pinches the bridge of his nose and closes his eyes, letting out a slow breath.

Jett steps forward, his broad shoulders back, cutting a tall and imposing figure as he points at the reluctant pair. A thrill of desire courses through me at the sight of him, his strong, muscular frame clearly visible through his well-fitted suit.

"If you didn't want to come, you should have damn well said!" he barks. "Now you're wasting everyone's time, mine especially!"

He glances apologetically at me, seeming to regret his words. I smile back. His gaze lingers on me for a moment, and I can't help but enjoy the attention.

"There's one way we can resolve this," Lyle says. He pulls a cell phone from his jacket pocket. "We insist. I'm sure if we speak to someone at HQ, we can come to an agreement, and get clearance for a quick, quiet helicopter tour."

He looks at me, eyebrows raised. He waggles the cell phone at me.

"What do you say, Casey? Do you think they'd appreciate the call? I don't think it would go down too well, you refusing the request from the very person who started the whole project in the first place."

I shrug. I glance at Jett. His expression is incredulous, and his face flushed with anger.

"First of all, Lyle," I respond calmly. "Headquarters doesn't call the shots here. *I* do. Oh, and good luck getting any reception. Most of this reserve is a cell phone deadzone. Nearest place I've found reception is about two hour's fast ride from here."

He looks at his phone, a forlorn expression coming over his features.

"Now, I'm going to have to insist," I continue, looking at the visitors in turn. "You've wasted enough of my time as it is. You have two options; come with me to see first hand what I do, or leave."

I gesture at the truck and the horses.

"I can take three of you in the truck, which I'd rather not use, or one of you on horseback," I add. "Though none of you are really dressed for such an expedition."

Lyle glances at Jett, and then back to me.

"Well, I think we're done here," he says, clearly annoyed. "Jett?"

He looks to his boss for support, but can't meet his gaze.

"Lyle," he says. "If you ever try any shit like that again, I'll fire you on the spot. Do you understand? Good, now what did I say when you asked about the helicopter before?"

"You said no helicopter - "

"That's right. That is what I said. So don't try and threaten someone for doing their damn job."

He turns to face me.

"And no, I'm not done here," he continues. "Casey, if you'll have me, I'd be honored to join you for the day. My team can go to the presentation without me, and return to pick me up on the way through tomorrow. What do you say?"

Oh god I want to say yes. To get you to myself. Just me and you, out in the wilderness. But...where did that thought come from? And can this pretty boy handle it? Wait for a moment before you respond. Don't seem too keen...

"Hmm," I say, pretending to be deep in thought. "Well, I've got a lot to do, and we'll be riding far. I'll most likely be staying out in the reserve overnight, as it will be too far to come back before nightfall.

"But, I have tents, sleeping bags, and more than enough supplies for the both of us."

I study his immaculate suit, and his soft leather shoes.

As if reading my thoughts, he holds his rucksack out and waves it at me.

"Unlike the others, I came prepared," he says, with a warm smile.

I can't help but be impressed. Part of me starts to believe that he genuinely cares, and I'm intrigued to see how he'll fare out on the plains.

"Right, you heard the man," Lyle says. "I'm sure we can handle a simple presentation without our illustrious, cowboy wanna-be leader."

"We'll come back for you tomorrow, early afternoon," he adds. "You'll be back by then, I trust?"

I nod, not taking my eyes off of Jett.

"Yes. Oh, and make sure you follow the exact route out of the reserve I've given you. Head south; the nearest herd is to the north, and there's another a way out to the north-east."

He waves away my concerns, and he and the rest of his cronies make their way back to the waiting helicopter.

"Yeah, the pilot's got your routes Don't worry, Mister Taylor. Enjoy the ride."

Oh I will. I'm sure I will. Whatever type of riding it is I end up doing...

CHAPTER THREE

JETT

The helicopter blades start up in a whirr and I turn to wave patronizingly at my departing colleagues as they head off for the city. After a while the vehicle disappears into the distance, and I take a moment to study my surroundings.

I take in a deep breath of the fresh country air, and almost immediately begin to feel at peace with my sudden remoteness. I feel something brush against my leg, and glance down to see Ted, sitting contently beside me, staring out into the field, as if trying to follow my gaze. I reach down to scratch the scrawny three-legged dog behind his ear before turning to head back towards the cabin.

Casey is already preparing the horses, loading up saddle bags and tying on tents and sleeping bags to the docile animals.

"Need a hand?" I ask, and he glances at me briefly over his shoulder, as if suddenly remembering my presence.

"Almost done here," he replies. "You can get changed in the cabin. Oh, and there's a blue rucksack with food and a cooler on the dining room table, if you could bring those out for me."

I simply nod and head in through the front door of the cabin, Casey's dog trotting obediently along beside me.

I change out of my suit quickly, and into the brand new clothes I'd bought especially for the trip. I suddenly feel a little silly at the bright, untarnished denim of my expensive jeans, the gleam of my new, heavy leather boots, and the folds in my heavy flannel shirt from where my housekeeper had ironed the damn thing, like she did almost everything else.

I keep the knife, multi-tool, thick woolen jumper and raincoat in my bag, and pick up the supplies from the table before heading back out, hefting the heavy bag of food over one shoulder with ease, and tucking the cooler under my right arm.

Casey watches me as I approach, and his tough guy facade cracks slowly as he studies me. Then, he bursts out laughing. The sound is almost musical, and infectious. Despite my frown of confusion, I can't help but smile back at him.

"I'm glad I amuse you," I say through my grin.

He shakes his golden mane, trying to suppress his laughter.

"I'm sorry, Jett," he replies. "It's just you like like you've stepped right out of *Cowboy Weekly*."

I hold out the heavy bag of supplies with one arm, trying both to show off, and to show him I won't be completely useless. My muscles bunch under the strain, but I hold the bag steady.

I watch him as he studies the muscles of my arm and chest, bunching under my shirt. His eyes widen, and he takes the bag from me with two hands.

"What about your dog? Ted, I mean?" I ask. He smiles up at me as he loads the supplies, spreading them over a few saddle bags on both horses.

"There's a dog-flap that only opens for his collar. Keeps the feral cats and racoons out. I've left him plenty of food, and even on three legs he's nimble and clever enough to outsmart any bears that wander too close," he says, in a matter of fact tone.

"He'll probably follow us for a few miles, then head back to the lodge. He's -"

"Bears?" I say, a little worried.

He chuckles, and pats a rifle holster tied to the side of his horse, within hands reach when riding.

"Don't worry city boy. I'll keep you safe," he says patronizingly.

"As long as you're a good shot. How many could you get off with a bolt action rifle at a charging bear? Two, maybe three max?" I say as Casey walks over to lock the door of the cabin.

He jumps up onto his horse, and gestures for me to follow suit. I leap into the saddle fairly easily, and take up the reins. The horse is an old mare, sturdy and docile, and lets me pull on the reins without complaint as I guide her to follow along next to Casey as we head off out into the wilderness.

"Don't worry," he says. "Part of my job is to track and monitor black and grizzlies that pass through, or come down from the mountains. Most stay well away as soon as they catch the scent of a human, and there won't be any protective mothers with young cubs this time of year."

I glance from the trail to Casey as the horses plod alongside one another. The trail is narrow, and our thighs brush against each other briefly on occasion. If he notices the touch, he doesn't show it.

"Sounds like you got a lot to do out here then, Casey," I say.

He glances at me with a brief smile, and winks. A thrill runs through me as our eyes meet.

"Well, I'm glad someone appreciates it. There is a lot to do, mainly tracking and monitoring the mustang herds, and trying to keep them within the reserve."

He talks as we ride, and I find him easy to listen to. He's knowledgeable and passionate, and seems to appreciate the genuine interest I'm showing in his work.

Ted appears from a patch of scrub to one side of the trail, and jogs alongside the horses for a while.

"So you found him in the city?" I ask, nodding at the dog. "What happened?"

Casey glances at the dog, his expression softening.

"Like I said, he was hit by a car. I found him by the side of the road, a few months before I was due to come out here. I couldn't leave him there, so I took him to a vet, got him fixed up. It was touch and go for a while, but he recovered well, and I decided to bring him with me."

"That was well after my time then," I say absently, my mind wandering back to my veterinarian days.

Casey looks at me, confused.

"You used to be a vet?" He asks, incredulous.

I smile weakly. Everyone these days sees me as a billionaire businessman, and not as my true love, caring for animals, which I'd had to leave behind when my business took off.

"I used to own a practice in the city. I was happy enough, making decent money. Then, almost overnight, everything changed. Me and a few of my guys developed a range of pet care products, both cosmetic and medical, and, well, it sort of snowballed from there."

I cast my mind back to those early days, when we were naive and didn't realize how far the business would go in such a short time.

"I had to leave the practice behind, and concentrate all of my efforts on the business. I was... ruthless, focused on making a fortune. I forgot what really drove me for a while. Now, it seems, it's coming back to me. What really matters."

I sigh. It was true. I was fed up with the corporate life-style, and the stresses of being a CEO of a huge company. I felt *tired*.

"Well, thanks for sharing. I mean it, I never knew. And anyway, Jett, it's never too late. Remember that," Casey says in a matter of fact tone.

You know what, I think you're right. I don't have to be stuck in the boardroom, or kissing the assess of potential clients, or getting my employees out of trouble. I've made my fortune. Maybe it's time for me to step aside.

"So… there's no Mrs. Baxter back home?" Casey asks furtively.

I look over at him, to see him blushing a little. He looks away, seeming to regret asking the question.

"No. Not really my style. Besides, like I said, I've just been too focused on the business to care about anything else," I reply simply, trying to put him at ease without being too direct.

"How about you?" I ask.

"I don't date women. But in another way I've been the same," he responds. "Focusing on work more than anything else. Plus, I don't think many men would be too keen on their boyfriend or husband disappearing into the wilderness for months on end."

I shrug.

"Well, unless he worked with you," I reply.

We carry on in a comfortable silence for a moment. Since we left the cabin, we've been traveling along a path cutting through woodland and shrubland. Suddenly, the path opens out into a wide track, heading out onto a huge, open prairie.

"Wow," I say in awe, dumbstruck by the scale of the reserve.

Casey points out into the distance, where I can just make out a herd of mustang, faint brown blobs from this distance.

"They stayed!" he exclaims, clearly excited. "OK. We're going to approach the herd, so I can make an assessment of numbers, and check to see if and how many foals there are. Follow me, calm and slow."

We head out into the prairie, and the excitement is palpable from Casey, as he takes out a clipboard and a pair of binoculars. He's engrossed in his work, and I suddenly realize that I'm staring at him, taking in the plains and swells of his body as he rocks gently from side to side on his horse.

I try to suppress the thoughts and desires rising strong within me at his proximity, vainly trying to brush aside a picture of him in my mind's eye, as I slowly unbutton his shirt, and pull his jeans down from his strong, athletic thighs...

He catches me looking, glancing at me sideways. I glance away, but a look in him tells me the attention wasn't exactly unwanted.

And it's just going to be us two, alone, out under the stars. Let's hope I'm not imagining this chemistry I can feel between us.

I bring myself back to the present, and try to focus on the task at hand, rather than the body of this beautiful young man riding along beside me.

CHAPTER FOUR

CASEY

I've been pleasantly surprised by Jett over the course of the day, and the negative stereotype I'd formed of him before I'd even met him had quickly been dispelled. He's clever, witty and attentive. And damn, is he sexy.

I was pretty sure I even caught him checking me out on a few occasions, when he thought I was focusing on something else. Men seem to zone out and lack self awareness when their eyes wander, and have a sixth sense when it comes to eyes roaming my body.

Still, I can't help but enjoy the attention, and the chemistry between us is obvious now, and getting stronger by the minute.

We've just finished scouting the mustang herd and the surroundings, and before we know it the day had all but passed. There's an electricity in the air, and dark, ominous storm clouds appearing on the horizon.

"We'd better go set up camp," I say, my voice having to strain a little over the strong wind rolling across the open prairie.

"Those clouds don't look too good," Jett responds, and I'm once again impressed by how observant he is of our natural surroundings.

I start to lead my horse away from our vantage point, a grass knoll far out in the center of the prairie, and head towards the distant tree line.

Jett pulls his horse up alongside me, his masculine scent and the smell of his aftershave wafting towards me. I inhale deeply, feeling a long suppressed stirring of sexual desire rise within me.

I have to remind myself, again, that this guy is effectively my boss. Any sort of intimate relationship would likely be inappropriate. Also, I am not one hundred percent certain that he is even gay. I try to brush aside my thoughts and desires, to no avail.

It's only me and him out here. No one else. And if he feels the same way, what's stopping us? Well, assuming he feels the same way, that is. I can't exactly jump on him this evening, if he doesn't. That would be an awkward ride back to the cabin tomorrow.

"I know a good spot where we can set up camp," I say, distracting myself with conversation. "A clearing in the woods. I've spent the night there a few times before."

I look over my shoulder at the dark storm clouds.

"Well, not exactly in these circumstances," I add with a chuckle. "But I'm sure we'll be just fine."

"I don't know about you," Jett replies. "But I'm starving. Let's hope we can get a fire set up before the rain comes down, eh?"

I look over to nod at him, and his dark, handsome eyes lock on mine.

I should have told him I only had one tent. Or I could say we need to share. For warmth, of course...

Before long we're at the tree line, and I lead my horse first along a narrow track that I know opens out into a big clearing after a short distance. I'd only recently scouted these woods and there was no recent sign of any bears. The browns never strayed this far from the mountains, and the grizzlies are rare in these parts, especially in the patchy woodland dotted around the prairies.

We set up camp, hitching the horses to a tree stump, and tying some tarpaulin over them between four trees to give them cover from the impending rain. They would be comfortable enough as long as we kept the rain off of them. Thunder and lightning could startle them, I know, but I make sure they're tied securely, brushed down and fed.

Jett deftly hitches his tent, cleverly deciding to tie the guy ropes to some nearby trees. I follow suit, and before long the camp is set up, and we throw our bedding into our respective tents.

We both help with setting up a fire, inside the ring of stones I set up on my first overnight visit to the clearing. I watch as Jett sets the kindling almost expertly under the larger logs, and blows big lungfuls of air at the fledgling fire. After a moment it's a roaring flame, and takes the edge off of the chill wind blowing through the trees.

Jett sees me watching him work, and he smiles a knowing smile at me.

"Scouts," he says, as if reading my thoughts. "So, what's for dinner, chef?" he asks with a wink.

I head over to grab a few supplies from the saddle bags I've hitched up on a tree, and grab the cooler.

"Tonight," I say, brandishing the supplies with a flourish. "I'll be serving steaks with BBQ beans. A woodland delicacy."

I settle a metal frame over the fire, and place a pan on top. I open the cooler, and take out two bottles of beer, which I'm happy to find are still cold.

"And I think we deserve these, after our day's work," I add, and pass him a beer.

We twist off the tops, and clink our bottles together. Our eyes meet as we swig from the bottles, Jett's sparkling bright, reflecting the glow of the fire.

"So, tell me about your veterinarian practice," I ask, as I set about cooking our dinner.

Jett tells me about his old life, before his business took off and he made his fortune. He tells me he was happier then, when things were more simple, and he longs to return to a similar life one day.

He surprised me by saying that he could see himself doing something similar to what I'm doing out here, being so close to nature, enjoying the peace and tranquility. He also says he wants to give something back, hence the charitable foundations and nature reserves he's set up.

After we've eaten, our conversation is interrupted by an ominous crash of thunder, rolling in a deep rumble over the prairie, and into the woods. We glance at each other, and rise to our feet, as the rain starts coming down through the trees.

We stand there, eyes locked, the rain increasing in intensity. I want to bring him to me, to hold him close, to feel his lips against mine. But I can't move. For the first time in god knows how long, I'm nervous. Doubts start to fill my mind.

Then he steps forwards and places his big hands on my waist. His eyes search mine for approval, for permission. I half close my eyes, and let my head tilt to the side, bringing my mouth towards his.

As our lips brush together, a rash of lightning sounds nearby, making both of us jump and panicking the horses.

I reluctantly pull myself away from the warmth of Jett's body.

"I should…" I shout over the noise of the storm.

He nods in acceptance, and jerks his thumb towards his tent. The moment has gone, suddenly, and I inwardly curse this damn, interrupting storm.

I nod back, with a disappointed sigh, and go to tend to the horses.

nother crash of lightning rouses me from a fitful sleep. The rain is intense, pattering heavily against the waterproof canvas of my tent. The horses whinny in loud panic, and I rise to sit, and pull my boots on.

I rush out from the tent to find the horses' hitching post has come loose, the stump coming free from the drenched soil. I run over to make sure they don't bolt, and calm then both with soothing whispers and pats on their snouts.

A figure emerges from the darkness. Jett. Shirtless, only wearing jeans and his boots. Rain glistens on his skin, taut over his muscled torso. He runs over to help me with the horses, and we tie them to a tree this time, and make sure the tarpaulin is secure.

The horses seem to have calmed with our presence, and we leave them to head back to the tents. I glance down at myself, suddenly remembering what I'm wearing. My thin undershirt is soaked, my nipples are hard and the swells of my pecs are clearly visible through the wet material.

I shake the rain out of my hair and head back to my tent. I stop suddenly, realizing I've left the tent flap open. The inside of my tent is pooling with rain water. Luckily my clothes are in a waterproof bag, but all of my bedding looks soaked.

I feel an arm around my waist, and glance up to see Jett. His body is pressed against mine, the warmth of his torso seeping through to my naked body under my thin night clothes.

He pulls me towards his tent, and I follow without complaint. Luckily he'd thought to close the flap of his tent, and he gestures for me to enter. I climb in, slipping out of my boots and sitting down on the foot of his bedding.

He enters after me, and closes the tent behind him. Another crash of lightning, almost immediately followed by thunder, lights up the tent for a moment.

I lean over to talk in Jett's ear, above the din of the storm.

"I'm soaked!" I half shout. "I'm going to have to... before we..."

His eyes widen, and he nods. He gestures at his wet jeans, and shrugs.

Jett turns away from me, and I pull my soaked shirt from my body. My boxer shorts follow suit. I'm naked underneath, but instead of feeling embarrassed, I feel empowered. And incredibly horny. I'm already semi hard.

I shuffle back to the sleeping back. But I don't get inside. I lie there, resting on my elbows, my legs crossed at the ankle, waiting for Jett to turn around.

After pulling his jeans off, he turns around and freezes in surprise as his eyes drift over my naked body. He pauses for a moment, and I gesture him forward with a finger, longing to feel his naked body pressed against mine.

CHAPTER FIVE

JETT

I'd been unable to sleep, cursing myself for not acting on the chemistry I'd felt between us, as we'd both hesitated to turn in for the night. The sudden arrival of the storm and the need for Casey to calm the horses had dispelled the moment, however, and I'd reluctantly gone back to my tent, alone.

But now I found myself sat at the foot of my sleeping bag, wearing only my boxer shorts, studying the naked body of Casey, as he gestures for me to join him on the inflatable mattress. His still wet skin glistens in the night's gloom, and I can just about make out the tantalizing muscles of his full body.

I edge forward towards him until I'm alongside him on top of the sleeping bag. My naked torso brushes against his, and I feel myself start to swell with desire. I glance down at Casey. A flash of lightning lights up the tent for a second, revealing his naked body.

His eyes are on mine, bright and inviting, his lips parted slightly. The sight of his strong chest, broad and sunburnt, and his dark, hard nipples turns me on even more. I feel my member swell, and it starts to press hard against the skin of his thigh.

He smiles knowingly at me, and I lean in to him, slowly bringing my mouth to his. Our lips brush for a moment, and then I press my mouth hard against his. His breath is warm against my cheek, the scent of his woodsy smell filling my senses as we kiss.

I open my mouth to caress his tongue with mine, and he lets out a little groan of pleasure. I push my body against his, pressing my hard erection against him. I place a hand on his chiselled abs, caressing his skin gently before sliding my hand down to grasp his already hard cock.

His dick is heavy and swollen, almost filling my large hands as I stroke him gently, feeling the ridge of his head brush against my palm. I flick at his nipple with my tongue, and nibble it gently between my teeth. He groans again, and his body squirms next to mine.

I gasp as he reaches to grab my cock through my boxer shorts, holding the shaft tight as he jerks me off, slow yet firm. I close my eyes for a moment, enjoying the sensation of pleasure at the touch of his warm hand on me.

Casey opens his legs suggestively, lifting his knees to either side of his body. Another flash of lightning illuminates the tent. I catch a tantalizing glimpse of his ass, bubble shaped, blond pubic hair reflecting in the light before darkness returns.

I run my hand down his body, slowly over the skin of his lower stomach, caressing the thick tangled tuft of hair above his sex, before sliding my middle finger toward his ass. He's warm, and incredibly tense, and I massage his hole gently with my middle finger, increasing my pressure ever so slowly.

His back arches and he moans into my mouth as I pleasure him, running my finger in slow circles around his sensitive hole. He leans in to me to pull at the elastic of my boxer shorts, and with my free hand I obligingly pull them down and kick them away.

My rock hard erection springs free from the tight confines of my underwear, and I feel Casey's hand run from the base of my shaft along to the tip, squeezing at me, trying to get a measure of my length and girth. Then, he grabs my shaft just under my glans, and jerks me off hard and fast, as if in desperation.

I thrust my hips forward in time with the movement of his hand, pressing my cock against his rough skin as he jerks me off. I groan loud at the pleasure building within me, and shudder at the sensation.

I press two fingers against his opening, teasing him for a moment before pushing one into his ass. He's tight, but slicked with sweat, and my finger slides into him easily. I push it in as far into him as I can, reaching for his prostate.

We lie there for a long moment, pleasuring each other with our hands, our naked bodies pressed against one another. Then, he takes his hand from my shaft and presses at my shoulder, and I obligingly lie down onto my back.

Casey sits up for a moment to reverse the direction he's lying in, and he lies back down on his side, pressing his body against mine. He props his head up on one hand, and takes my cock into his hand again.

Casey studies my member for a moment as he jerks me off slowly, his eyes glistening and hungry as he studies my throbbing cock. Then, he takes me into his mouth, his warm tongue lapping at my glans in time with the movement of his hand.

His own cock is close to my face now, giving me a better view despite the dim light. The sight of his uncircumsized member, just as hard as my own, turns me on even more. I take him into my own mouth and relish the feeling of his smooth head gliding over my wet lips.

I reach around and grab his thick ass and pull his body toward me, leaning to bring my mouth closer and closer to the base of his shaft. Then I vibrate my tongue to tease his glans, as my now dripping wet fingers search again for his asshole.

I feel Casey take my cock deep into his mouth, and his lips close around me. He moans loud around my shaft as he sucks at me. He cups my balls with his free hand, squeezing them gently in time with the movement of his tongue, as he runs it in circles around the sensitive tip of my cock.

His chest presses against my stomach as he rocks back and forth, his hard nipples grazing my skin as he pleasures me with his mouth. I gasp as I feel my cock twitch in pleasure, and he slows down suddenly, pulling my erection out of his mouth.

He kisses along the length of my shaft, holding me in one hand, and I shudder at the sensation of his full lips brushing gently against the skin of my cock.

I watch him as he kisses me, my mouth still suckling on his cock, my face covered with my own saliva. I suck at his head, and he gasps, frowning down at me in pleasure, watching me as I tease him.

I push his hips down so he's lying on his back, and he yelps in surprise as I sit up and grab him with strong arms, positioning him on his back in the middle of the tent.

Casey opens his legs invitingly, biting his lip as his eyes meet mine. I lower myself onto him, gently resting my body against his. I support my weight with one strong arm, and grab one of his thighs with my free hand, opening his legs wide.

I take my dripping wet erection in one hand and guide it towards him, slowly thrusting my hips forward. I pause for a moment, sliding the tip of my cock up into his asshole, working my way into him slowly, slowly feeling him stretch to accommodate me.

His body shudders at the touch, and I enjoy teasing him for a moment as he squirms and moans, his naked body lying ready and willing before me. I enjoy being in control, and this is no different.

I want him to beg me for it, to give in to his wildest animalistic desires before I let myself go, past the point of no return.

I slide myself in and out, enjoying the sensation of his warm, tight asshole against my cock. He's nice and wet from the blow job, his lips flushed and swollen with sexual desire.

I pull out and press myself gently against his opening, and he moans with frustration as I push my cock inside only briefly, before pulling back out again, teasing him even more.

"Jesus, Jett..." he moans, his voice strained and loud over the noise of the storm.

"Come here and fuck me. Fuck me hard," he continues, almost pleading.

A flash of lightning reveals his sculpted face, eyes half closed and his cheeks flushed red. He nods at me encouragingly, and takes my hips in his hands.

He tries to pull me forward, and I resist for a moment, his strength an even match for mine. Then, I give in to my desires, and push my cock into him.

I feel him stretch tight around my big, hard erection as I thrust slowly into him. I lean forward to press my body hard against his, his thick patch of chest hair scratching against the more bare skin of my own chest.

He gasps long and loud, shuddering as my full length slides into him, stretching him to the limit. Still, he pulls me forward, wanting to take all of me deep into him.

Casey bites the skin of my shoulder as I push the last of my length into his beautiful body, and I groan with pleasure at the sensation of his tight ass enveloping the entirety of me. I feel myself twitch a little, and my body shudders involuntarily.

There's an electricity in the air; from the storm, and from the strong sexual chemistry between us, and I feel it empower me. I start to fuck him, slow at first, making sure my considerable length and girth doesn't cause him too much pain.

But he shudders and groans in pleasure, his hands all over my hips and butt as he wills me to go faster, harder.

He moans in my ear, murmuring incoherent words of encouragement. Everything else is forgotten as I'm absorbed in the moment, the entirety of my senses filled with him, his smell, his skin pressed against mine, the warmth of his body.

I grab one of his thighs and bend his leg at the knee, pushing it up and to the side, allowing me to fuck him deep and fast. Our eyes lock for a moment, his face contorted into a mask of pleasure.

CHAPTER SIX

CASEY

Jett's gym toned body is pressed against mine, his manly scent strong as he moans in pleasure in my ear as he thrusts deep and hard into me.

The sensation of his huge, incredibly hard cock filling me is like nothing else I've ever experienced before, and the intense pleasure is almost painful. I claw at his back in desperation, willing him to thrust faster and harder, to push himself as deep into me as he can over and over again.

I start to shudder as pleasure shoots through my body, starting from my balls and coursing up into my cock, my stomach, and my sensitive nipples. I feel like my whole body is experiencing the sensation, and it's incredible.

He's grunting in time with his thrusts now, the noise animalistic and raw, his breath coming in hot gasps onto my neck. His moans of pleasure only serve to turn me on even more, and I feel an intense pressure start to build up in my body.

It's almost unbearable, and I moan and start to shudder. His incredibly hard, throbbing cock fills me again and again, stretching me to my limit as he fucks me. I grab his butt, feeling his muscles tense with every thrust.

The power of the storm outside the tent only serves to add to the electric energy between us, and the sex feels raw and powerful. The prostate orgasm takes me by surprise, and I scream loud as the inside of my ass convulses hard, clenching rhythmically.

Jett's eyes widen as they meet mine, and I claw at his back as I attempt to ride the wave of pleasure that's taking over my body. My whole body shudders and convulses, and my back arches involuntarily, pressing my naked body hard against his.

His thrusts slow, and he lets out a long, low groan and closes his eyes. Even as my orgasm starts to fade, I feel him start to come, his cock bunching and twitching powerfully inside me.

"Oh, fuck…" he moans into my ear, voice deep and strained with pleasure.

He shudders and his muscles tense as he orgasms, thrusting into me one final time and holding his cock fully inside of me. I feel his cum spurt into me again and again as he ejaculates powerfully, and I feel waves of pleasure and relaxation roll over me as he climaxes.

After a long moment his muscles relax, and his body is heavy on top of mine as the energy seeps from him. I grasp the hair at the back of his head and hold him close to me, our breathing deep and heavy as we recover our strength.

Consciousness returns to me slowly as I wake. The first thing that strikes me is the near silence; the storm has passed now, and the air is filled with the quiet sounds of the morning.

The second thing is the presence of a huge, warm body next to mine. I smile as the memories of last night come back to me, along with a warm glow of deep sexual satisfaction.

My head is resting on Jett's chest, rising and falling with his slow and steady breaths. I doze off for a peaceful moment before rousing myself from my slumber. I need to check on the horses, and survey the storm damage.

Also, if the forecasts from headquarters are correct, that wasn't the first, or the worst of the storms, and we had to get back to the ranger station as soon as we can to get the place repaired, if needed, and ready for a hurricane.

I try my best to rise from the bed as quietly as possible as to leave Jett resting for a little while longer, but he stirs as soon as my head leaves his chest. His eyes open slowly, and he looks around confused for a moment before his eyes settle on mine.

I sit up, uncaring of my nakedness, and his eyes drop to study my naked body.

"Good morning," he says, not taking his eyes from my body.

"Are you talking to me, or this?" I ask, cupping my erection in my hands and squeezing it.

His eyes widen at the gesture, and his face flushes with desire.

"Both," he replies, voice husky.

I turn away from him, and start to pull on my boots.

"Hold that thought," I say. "We need to get back to the ranger station as soon as we can. There'll be plenty of time for...us later. I doubt you'll be going anywhere for a day or two."

He sits up in the bed and rubs at his eyes.

"More storms due?" he asks as he shuffles his naked body from the sleeping bag.

It's my time to stare, his arousal at the sight of my naked body clearly evident for a moment before he pulls on his boxer shorts.

"Last time I called in to HQ, yeah," I reply as I open the tent flap and rise, naked other than my boots, to my feet. "And worse to come yet."

"Let's get packed up," I continue as I study our surroundings. "If we ride fast we can be back before midday. No sightseeing today, I'm afraid."

There's still a slight chill in the morning air as I walk over to my tent, and my nipples stiffen in the breeze. A few branches litter the clearing, and out in the thin woodland surrounding us I can see a few uprooted trees. Nothing serious, which means the ranger station is likely in good shape, with a bit of luck.

I dress quickly into my clothes, suddenly glad I'd had the foresight to pack them into a waterproof bag. Then we both set about getting the camp packed away, and loaded onto the horses.

Before long we're trotting out through the woodland in single file, before opening the horses pace up into a canter as we clear the trees and head off back to the ranger station across the open prairie.

The sky is clear, and a cool breeze blows gently across the open grassland. The sun is out, and it's a fine day - if it wasn't for the occasional downed tree at the edge of the distant tree line, you'd be forgiven for not believing there had been a storm last night, and that more were on the way.

Jett and I ride in a comfortable silence, and we make good time with the horses riding at a steady trot. I'm impressed with his riding skills, though he freely admitted himself that he hasn't ridden since he was a teenager, and I can tell he's a little rusty.

I notice the occasional wince or a grunt as he mistimes his movement, and I can't help but smile, even though I feel a little bad at finding his discomfort amusing.

"You OK over there, cowboy?" I ask, after a particularly bad bump.

He finished the string of muttered curses and glances over at me with a pained smile.

"I'm good. Just getting a little... sore, down there. Yesterday was fine, but with this faster pace I'm finding it hard to keep in time with the horse," he replies.

"Well, just make sure you don't damage anything too much. I'm going to need you in working order later on. I mean, what else are we going to do when the hurricane blows in?"

He grins broadly at my words, perking up and forgetting about the pain as his mind wanders at my suggestive words.

"Oh, don't you worry Casey. Everything will work just fine, you'll see," he says happily.

I feel a thrill of sexual excitement run through me at his gaze, and tear my eyes away from him.

"You'll be pleased to hear we're almost there. See where the prairie narrows and the scrubland thickens into woodland? That's where we came out yesterday," I say, gesturing with a sweep of my arm.

Jett nods, recognition in his eyes as he surveys the landscape.

Before long we're on the final, well-beaten track that will take us to the edge of the clearing where the ranger station is. I'm almost holding my breath, worried about the state of the cabin, and the wellbeing of my three-legged companion.

I release my held breath at the sound of an excited bark, and a scraggy figure appears at the end of the path, charging towards us. Jett laughs happily at the appearance of Ted, and I smile with relief.

"Good to see you made it, boy," he shouts. "I hope you've kept the place safe!"

Ted follows us along as we reach the final curve of the path, his tail wagging madly as he keeps pace with the horses.

We turn the corner, and relief washes over me. The place is pretty much untouched. Everything that wasn't tied down outside is now strewn across the grass in front of the cabin, of course. But the structure is fine, and all of the windows are intact.

I glance at the stable, which has a few loose panels on one side, but looks structurally sound. We'd need to shore it up before the worst of the storm hit, but I have plenty of materials to fix the cabin and the stable up.

And I also have a strong, handsome helper to boot. I could get used to having someone here with me. Especially someone like Jett...

I brush the thought aside, and we set about taking care of the horses before starting work on fixing the place up.

CHAPTER SEVEN

JETT

It doesn't take too long to get the place "storm ready", as Casey calls it, with both of us working in tandem together. It turns out that we make a damn good team, and I make no complaint as he tells me what to do, enjoying not having to think or make the decision for once.

We shore up the stable, adding planks of wood to improve the strength of the structure, but removing a few panels strategically, to let the wind pass through rather than tear the frame down. The horses would be relatively dry and out of the worst of the storm, and Casey even had some warm, waterproof coats that would keep them from catching a chill.

The cabin takes a bit more work - we board up the windows and close the outer shutters, nailing them shut. Even the dog flap gets boarded up, just in case the dog gets excited and charges out into the storm, only to be blown or washed away.

We clear away or secure anything not fixed down outside of the cabin, and clear the debris strewn across the place from last night's storm. The bulk of the heavy work done, we stand outside of the cabin, surveying our handiwork.

"Looks pretty damned storm proof," I say, and Casey nods in agreement.

He glances at the solar panels, which look secure enough, designed to withstand hurricane force winds, then frowns at the radio antenna.

"I'm going to check in with HQ, then we need to take the antenna down or it's going to get busted," he says.

I follow him into the cabin, and he approaches the large radio station in the corner of the room.

Casey toys with a few dials and lifts the mouthpiece.

"Ranger Station Four to headquarters, come in, over," he says, the words sounding well-rehearsed.

There's a crackle of static before a voice responds, loud and clear.

"Headquarters here. How's it going out there, Casey? Take any damage from the storm, over?" A concerned female voice responds.

"Everything is A-OK out here, HQ. Any update on the forecast? And have you been in touch with Jett's team, over?"

Another crackle of static.

"Strong storms due any time now, for the next two days before they clear. Hurricane force winds are likely. Jett's team are holed up in the city, no pickup possible until the storms pass, over."

Casey glances over his shoulder at me with a warm smile. In truth, I want nothing more than to stay here with him, and I send out a silent prayer of thanks for the impeccable timing of these storms.

"Reading you loud and clear HQ. I'm going to secure radio antenna, so we will be out of contact until the worst of it passes, unless we get a clear window. We have plenty of supplies and will stay safe. Ranger station Four, out."

Casey switches off the radio and rises to his feet. He studies me for a moment, an unreadable expression on his boyish features.

"I'll go and secure the antenna. While I'm doing that, you bring in a few days' worth of wood for the fire, and give the outside of the cabin the once over, all right?" he says softly.

One thing's for sure, I quite like it when he bosses me around. Hopefully he'll be doing more of that, later. Touch me, Jett, here, just like this...

"On it!" I say enthusiastically, and give him a mock salute.

He taps me playfully on the chest as he passes, and my eyes follow his broad shoulders and bubble butt from the cabin.

The afternoon passes into evening as we finish our work, and we both start to relax, content the cabin is secure. Casey and I shower together, the excuse being to save the store of hot water, but we both enjoy it nonetheless.

We eat dinner together, enjoying the food over candlelight, relaxing in each other's company as if we've known each other for years.

One thing's for sure, despite my fear of attachment, I find my feelings growing strong for this unique and sexy man, strong yet elegant, shy, yet self-assured.

After we've eaten, Casey rises to go to a cupboard, and pulls out a slightly dusty wine bottle from the back.

"One of the girls at HQ bought me this as a good luck present," he says as he studies the label. "But I never found the right moment to open it."

He smiles up at me.

"Until now," he adds.

I rise to my feet and smile back.

"You open the wine, and I'll get a fire going," I say, and head to the fireplace.

The wind is starting to howl outside, the noise muffled somewhat by the thick wooden walls of the cabin. Despite the approaching storm, I feel safe and comfortable, and in good company.

Casey joins me on the couch, the fire roaring away cheerfully in the large, open fireplace opposite us.

I take a glass from him gratefully, enjoying the taste of the rich red wine as I take a gulp. Casey sits lengthways on the couch, resting his feet on my lap. I take a blanket from behind me and throw it over us, placing a hand on his thigh, rubbing him gently through the thin material of his flannel pajama pants.

I can feel his eyes on me, and I glance over to him, holding his gaze. His skin is ruddy and I can see just the faintest crow's feet in the corners of his eyes in the dim light, and he looks Earthy and handsome. His lips are pursed in thought for a moment.

"Can I tell you something, Jett?" he asks thoughtfully.

I gesture for him to continue.

"Shoot," I reply with a smile.

He looks around at his surroundings for a moment, before looking back at me.

"I've always wanted to be a vet. In fact, that's the reason I'm here. I'm saving up so I can afford to take the training," he says. "I've dreamed of it since I was a kid, and at least this way I'm helping animals and the natural environment even before I follow my dreams."

His voice is hesitant and quiet, as if he's not opened up to anyone for a long time, if at all.

I sigh thoughtfully.

"Truth be told, I never wanted to stop being a vet," I admit, the words coming unbound from my mouth. "So many times over the years, especially recently, I've thought about it, a few times even coming close to walking away from my role as CEO."

Casey sips at his wine, eyes sparkling as he listens intently.

"Sure, the money is great. But what else have I got? It's a cliché, I know, but money doesn't buy you happiness. Comfort and security, sure, but if you chase it seeking happiness, you'll likely be disappointed. Well, I that's what I've found anyway," I continue.

I've never opened up like this, not to anyone, since my mother passed away all those years ago. Before the money, and the relative fame. When life was simpler, and before I'd become arrogant and insular, to protect myself from those I didn't truly trust.

"Well, why don't you?" Casey says softly after a moment of silence.

I frown at him momentarily, distracted from my memories.

"Why don't I what?" I ask.

He shrugs.

"What's stopping you from stepping down from your role? You've made your money. You still have a stake in the company, right? One thing my dad always told me; no one is indispensable. What if, god forbid, something happened to you, to us, tonight? The company would go on. Maybe even thrive.

"You deserve to be happy, Jett, is all I'm saying. I say screw those that object, do what you truly want. I mean, you can handpick your replacement right? Hand over to and advise him, or her, personally? I can see it working, anyway."

Casey pauses for a moment, looking a little flushed.

"Sorry if I'm overstepping the line here. I'm just spit balling here, seeing what I see. And wine always loosens my tongue," he adds, with a grin.

His words have instilled something inside of me, a confidence, and I don't regret him speaking. I want to thank him for his candor, in fact.

"Don't mention it. I'm glad it's not just me that thinks it. Well, I've got time to think over the next day or so, right?" I reply.

I take another sip of wine, and I feel a stirring of desire at Casey's words. My eyebrows raise and I smile suggestively at him.

Wine always loosens my tongue...

I gesture at the almost empty glass in his hand.

"Loosens your tongue, eh? Why don't you come here and show me how loose it is?" I say, voice hoarse with desire.

His eyes widen for a moment, and then a matching dirty smile spreads on his lips. He takes our glasses and places them on the coffee table before us, approaching me across the couch slowly on his hands and knees.

The smell of his freshly washed hair wafts over me, and I breathe the scent in deep. An image of his naked body enters my mind, and I feel my cock stiffen with the anticipation of seeing it once again.

I turn to face him, and he sits next to me, his legs bent underneath him. His chest is level with my eyes, and I can just make out the outline of his strong pecs under his t-shirt.

Casey leans down to kiss me, pressing his full lips hard against mine. I brush my hand softly over the stubble skin of his cheek, and he smiles at the gesture.

"You're gorgeous, Casey," I whisper, and he kisses me harder, more desperately, pressing his body against mine.

CHAPTER EIGHT

CASEY

Jett's words send a tingle of pleasure through me, running along my spine and down into the pit of my stomach. I can feel the warmth of his body seeping through my thin clothes, the solid muscles of his chest pressed hard against the burning skin of my own chest.

I reach down to tug at the hem of his shirt, and pull it up over his head. I lean back a little to admire his smooth skin, taught over well-defined pectoral muscles and washboard abs.

Jett lifts his arms up to pull his shirt off, and throws it to one side. I lean down to run my tongue across his body, starting at his abs and working my way up to his neck. He moans gently as my tongue caresses his skin.

I glance down at his pants. The bulge of his swelling erection is easy to make out, and a thrill of sexual excitement courses through me at the thought of his big, erect manhood, and how it had felt inside me.

My hands are a little shaky as I fumble with his pants, and he helps me to pull them down. I grab the hem of his boxers and they soon follow his pants to the floor.

His cock stands proud, long and hard, and I take it in my hand. My fingers curl themselves around the girth of his shaft. I start to jerk him off, enjoying the sensation of his rock hard erection against the skin of my hand.

He groans in pleasure, and I glance up at him, and our eyes meet. His face is flushed with pleasure, and his eyes half close as I tug hard at his cock. With my free hand I cup his large balls, and squeeze gently in time with the movement of my other hand, feeling him twitch at the sensation of my warm hands on him.

Jett's cock is incredibly hard, swollen and twitching with pleasure at my touch. I suddenly take my hands from him, and slowly rise to my feet to stand in front of him.

He watches me as I slowly undress, lifting my t-shirt to slowly reveal my bare chest underneath. He gently strokes his cock as he watches, his eyes roving my body as he pleasures himself at the sight of me undressing.

I pull my shirt over my head and drop it to the floor. I run my hands over my chest and my neck, tense with excitement, pouting suggestively and twisting my hard nipples between thumb and forefinger.

I run my hands flat against my stomach, and tuck my fingers into the elastic of my pants. My eyes are on his, and I hold his gaze as I slowly pull my pants down my thighs, letting my already rock hard cock spring free, and I bend down to push the pants to my feet.

After stepping out of my pants I take a step forward, standing before him fully naked. I place my feet in a wide stance, and run a hand over my stomach, and start to stroke myself as he watches.

I'm incredibly hard, so I get my fingers slick with saliva as I caress my glans slowly in a circular motion, sending waves of pleasure shooting through me. I squeeze my left nipple with my free hand, letting out a soft moan of pleasure.

Jett squirms on the couch before me, jerking himself off faster now, his eyes wide with sexual frustration as I touch my body so close to him. The sight of his engorged member turns me on even more, and it takes all of my self-control to stop myself from jumping on him, and forcing his cock deep into me.

. . .

I decide to tease him for a little longer, knowing the pleasure will be that much greater for both of us, increased by anticipation. I grab the cheek of my own ass, and smack it so it jiggles for him, mimicking the way it would shake if he were pounding against me, I'm so turned on.

I move to kneel on the couch, placing one leg on either side of Jett's. I shuffle forward to bring myself so I'm perched just above his massive erection, my cock bouncing gently as I move.

I slide the drawer on the end table open and produce a bottle of lube, handing it over to him without a word.

"I'm ready for you, Jett," I whisper.

He slicks himself up for me and places a hand on my waist, urging me to lower my hips and to push him into me. I resist for a moment before obliging, and I slowly settle down into him.

He holds his cock, guiding it towards my opening as I lower my body. I shudder with pleasure as his glans touches my still tender from last time asshole, and slowly enters my channel. He thrusts up with his hips as I lower myself further, and my hole stretches around his thick manhood.

I use my two hands to stretch my ass cheeks apart, allowing him to slide into me a little easier, I close my eyes and moan his name as he fills me up, stretching me to my limit. I long to take his entire length inside of me.

I let out a soft groan of pleasure as my thighs and butt settle into his lap. He's fully inside me now, thrusting upwards with his hips to push his cock deep into me. I feel his cock twitch against the sensitive skin of my innermost wall, and pleasure courses through me.

I start to ride him, slowly at first, sliding my lubed up butt up and down his thick shaft. I ride his entire length, from his balls to the tip of his glans, stopping for a moment as he's almost fully out of me, then thrusting downwards to drive him hard and fast into me.

His deep, regular moans of pleasure and the look of sexual frustration and desire on his face turns me on even more, and I resist the urge to ride him hard and fast, to feel him come inside me.

I slowly start to build up the pace as I fuck him, my movements fast and decisive, no longer slow and teasing. I start to lose control as waves of pleasure spread through my body, sending an electric tingling from my prostate through my stomach and up through my back.

A pressure builds in the pit of my stomach, and the pleasure builds in intensity as I ride him hard and fast, my thighs, cock and butt all slapping against his hard muscles as his cock is thrust into me, again and again.

A whimper of pleasure escapes my lips and I clench my eyes shut against the almost painful pleasure of climax as I start to orgasm, my whole body shaking and my sphincter clenching hard and rhythmically around his hard cock.

"Fuck, Jett," I say through clenched teeth. "I'm coming!"

He breathes in sharply and grunts at my words, holding my lower back to support me with his strong hands as the orgasm sweeps over me. I struggle to move, to continue fucking him, losing control of my body momentarily. He thrusts up into me, lifting my whole body up with the movement of his hips, pushing hard with his legs.

He's grunting hard and fast now, the noise almost animalistic, and I can tell, through the waves of pleasure, that he's lost control, my own orgasm driving him over the edge. He comes hard inside me, shuddering and gasping through clenched teeth as his warm cum spurts deep into me.

"Oh, fuck…" Jett says, his voice strained.

Our eyes meet, his half-closed with pleasure as we ride our own waves of pleasure together, our two different but equally mind blowing orgasms mingling as our bodies shudder against one another.

I gasp for air as the orgasm fades, my belly tingling as his cock twitches again and again, bunching hard inside me.

He gives one final push deep into me, then rests back into the couch, his cum all spent inside of me, mine dripping down both of our stomachs. I sag forward, resting my body against his as we breathe fast and deep, recovering our energy.

After a moment I feel his hand gently caress my hair, his fingers running over the stubble on my cheek. I look up into his eyes, and they sparkle bright, reflecting the light of the open fire behind me.

He smiles a satisfied smile, and kisses me gently on the lips.

"I think we're going to need another shower," he says with a smile.

Jett rises to his feet, slipping from inside me, and I laugh with amusement as he carries me through to the shower room, the sounds of the storm raging outside making me feel incredibly safe and comfortable in our little sanctuary.

CHAPTER NINE

JETT

I leave Casey snoring peacefully in his bedroom, his dog curled up at the foot of the bed. I figure it's early, but with the boarded windows it's hard to tell what time it is. I feel refreshed and awake regardless, and quietly make my way for a quick wash before taking a look around the inside of the cabin.

There's no storm damage, despite the fierce winds we'd heard the previous night. The fire has died down to embers, and the store of firewood is a little low. I heat up some water to make a coffee, and as I'm waiting for the pot to boil, my mind drifts to the advice Casey had given me last night.

Inside, I know, I've already made my decision. I've been longing for a way out for so long, and now I felt like I had the drive to do it. For me, for Casey, to bring us closer together when this whirlwind romance of our first meeting met its inevitable end.

I'm starting to formulate a plan, one which includes the both of us. I feel a pang of apprehension about putting my heart on the line, but deep down I know there's a connection between us, something that will go places.

My coffee made, I take up a seat at the rough wooden dining table and flick open the folder I'd been given by Lyle, to study before the planned sales pitch I had managed to avoid attending.

I glance over the pages briefly. Company history, then our core values, followed by extensive information on our products. Then, sales figures, market values, expected revenues short and long term. A brief, but colorful section of our charitable work, and a few, sordid sections on the reasons that drove us to invest so heavily in them.

With a sigh I close the folder, and sip at my coffee. The only part in the whole folder I feel strongly about are the final sections. The rest is almost meaningless, facts and figures, money, profit, sales.

My mind made up, finally, I drain the rest of my coffee and head outside to collect some more firewood. There's a pile of logs out in the wood store, but none have been chopped to a manageable size.

I take an armful of logs over to the chopping block, the heavy woodsman's axe we'd secured the night before tucked under a bicep.

The cool morning breeze brushes over the skin of my naked torso, invigorating me as I chop at the wood. I cut a few logs down into shards for kindling, and the rest in increasingly larger blocks, to build up the fire.

The work is therapeutic, and I'm in a trance as I bring the axe up, and swing it down in one fluid motion, the muscle of my arms bunching with each blow. Before long the wood is almost chopped to size, enough I figure for a day or so at least, and I feel good, having built up a sweat.

I pick up as much of the wood as I can in one armful, and carry it through into the cabin, my muscles benching at the weight. I feel rugged and powerful, half hoping that Casey is awake to see my heroics.

I step through into the cabin, and he's at the dining table, a frown on his face as she pores over the document. I'm disappointed that he doesn't look up.

"Good morning," I say cheerily. "That's a load of boring, corporate nonsense. Much better suited to send you to sleep, rather than to read first thing."

He doesn't respond for a moment, then he looks up at me, his expression icy.

. . .

"What is this, Jett?" he says quietly.

I walk over to him, concerned. He's got the page open towards the end. My heart skips a beat as I realize what he's reading.

Pictures of the animal testing one of our very first product producers had undertaken, without our knowledge. The pictures do look bad, I have to admit. Hairless horses and smaller animals. Sick and dying rabbits and mice.

"That's not what it looks like, I can - "

He cuts me off, rising to his feet and pushing the folder hard into my chest.

"You... you said you cared! That's cruel, Jett. Evil," he says, starting to pace the room like a caged tiger.

"And the *court-mandated* charitable investments!? How could you lie to me like that? I thought we... you could have at least *told the truth!*"

I raise my hands placatingly, trying to find the words. But he's visibly so angry, and I know anything I say will likely make things worse. I'm actually afraid that he might take a swing at me.

Instead he storms off suddenly and I think I catch him quickly wiping at tears pooling in the corners of his eyes.

"Just when I thought I'd found someone real. I never should have let you in. People always let you down," he continues as he collects a few meagre supplies and leaves the cabin.

I follow Casey outside, to watch him head to the stables. I glance up at the sky. Dark, ominous clouds are on the horizon. The next storm is coming in, and fast.

"Casey! Let me explain!" I shout after him. "You can't go out now, there's a storm coming!"

He appears from the stable, his face as dark and ominous as the sky.

"Either I go, or you go, Jett. I can't even stand to look at you," he says, his voice ragged.

My heart almost breaks at how upset he is. I shake my head as he leaves, his dog dutifully trotting along beside him, oblivious to the developing situation.

I sigh. I know that I need to at least let him calm down a little, if he will, that is, before following after him. I check what he's taken in his haste to leave. A few tins of basic food, some water. A raincoat and jacket, his jeans and boots.

But no tent. No source of heat or light. And any heavy rain is going to make tracking him next to impossible.

Shit.

I decide that I need to act now. The rain will hit within the next ten minutes or so, I guess, possibly sooner. I dress quickly, pulling my shirt on over my head, and throwing on a jacket and raincoat.

I grab a tent and some tarpaulin, and throw it next to the door. My heart starts to race with panic and concern as I grab some more food, torches and a guarded cooking stove, and shove them all into a large rucksack.

I quickly grab some more clothes for Casey and a first-aid kit, and gather everything together in my arms and rush out to the stable.

After a moment of rushed packing, I head back to secure the cabin before returning to the horse. It looks worried and fretful, and I know it's picking up on my agitation. I take a few moments to close my eyes and breathe deeply to calm myself, before untying the horse and climbing up onto the saddle.

"Easy now, girl," I say gently, patting the horse's neck. "Nothing to worry about. Let's go nice and easy."

She snorts in response, and lets me guide her from the stable. The hoof marks from Casey's horse are fresh and clearly visible in the wet earth, giving me a path to follow, and I set out on his trail.

His tracks follow, more or less, our route from the previous day. I manage to work the path out, despite our tracks being washed away by the heavy rain. Then, suddenly, his course changes abruptly, and the stride of the hoof marks increase.

He's opened his horse up into a trot, and then gallop, heading in the opposite direction we went previously. I curse, knowing that I'll easily get lost in unfamiliar terrain, especially if I lose his trail.

I grit my teeth with determination as the wind picks up, and spots of rain start to patter against the material of my raincoat.

"Come on, girl. Let's see what you can do," I say with encouragement, and kick the horse into a gallop, heading out over the prairie to follow Casey's trail as the rain starts to fall harder, stinging my face as we fly over the wet grassland.

CHAPTER TEN

CASEY

There's nothing I can do to stop the tears streaming down my face, mingling with the stinging rain that's being whipped into my face by the wind. I glance over my shoulder to see a distant figure following my trail.

I knew that he'd follow. But I just want to get away from him, to return to the solitude I've become so accustomed to. I couldn't bear the thought of another night spent alone in the cabin with Jett, after everything I'd found about him and his past.

Sure, he might have changed. But how could I trust him now?

Yes Casey, I love animals. I want nothing more than to return to my old life of caring for them. Oh, by the way, to make my fortune I tortured and killed lots of them. But look, I'm doing good things now, just like the government forced me to!

I shake my head with disbelief. I don't want to hear his excuses, or his reasons why, at the time, it was acceptable. Because it was *never* acceptable.

I'm starting to regret leaving in such a hurry, stupidly heading out into the wilderness with barely any food and no shelter. Sure, I could hastily put together a makeshift cover, but with the severity of the storm due to be intense, anything I have time to fashion before it hits would be next to useless.

My best bet is to head for some sort of natural shelter, like an escarpment or steep hill, somewhere not low lying that would stay relatively dry. At least I would be able to escape the wind, if nothing else.

I remember a place I'd come across when I'd first started exploring the land surrounding the ranger station, heading out in increasingly longer forays into the prairies, in awe at the size and scale of the landscape, and the wide variety of natural environments they contained.

As the rain continues to increase in intensity, the sky starts to darken with black clouds, obscuring the mid-morning sun. The land around me takes on an eerie aspect, gloomy, yet charged with the tangible power of the coming storm. Visibility steadily reduces as the sky darkens, and I struggle to make out familiar landmarks to guide me.

I start to lose track of time, and I realize that my horse is starting to tire a little. I slow down the pace, and glance over my shoulder. If Jett is still hot on my trail, there's no sign of him. I figure that perhaps he's keeping his distance, hoping that I'd be circling around to eventually head back to the cabin before the storm hits.

I feel a slight pang of guilt, knowing that Jett will become lost and disoriented if he loses my trail. If I'm struggling to make out my whereabouts, there's no way he'd be able to find his way back to the cabin.

Still, it's his choice to follow me out into the storm. If he was sensible he'd have turned back already, to leave me to my solitude.

I brush the guilt and concerns away. What he does is his choice, and he's likely much better equipped than me, having had more time to prepare compared to my panicked, angry escape.

I need to focus on finding shelter, and keeping as dry as possible. And soon. The rain is hammering down now, and the open grassland under my horse is starting to churn into mud as we pass over it.

I quickly look around, slowing my horse to a walk and squinting against the heavy rain. My spirit lifts at the sight of a familiar landmark - an outcrop of trees just about visible in the gloom, that I knew lead to a patch of woodland, within which I'd find the steep, rocky escarpment, and my shelter until the storm passes.

With my horse headed towards the cover of the trees, I glance over my shoulder, looking out into the dark prairie I've just crossed. A flash of lightning illuminates the landscape, momentarily revealing a distant figure on horseback, laden with supplies, ten minutes or so behind me.

Damn you, Jett. Well, I can't risk going any further out into this. If he decides to follow me, he better have bought a tent, because he sure isn't sharing my shelter with me.

A loud clap of thunder rolls across the land, shaking the ground. The worst of the storm is approaching, I know, likely to hit in the next few minutes.

Before long I'm at the tree line, and slowly lead my horse under the canopy of the outlying trees. The woodland provides blessed relief from the wind and stinging rain, the wind lessening further as we head deeper inside.

I curse myself for not bringing a torch, and guide my horse carefully around obstacles in the ground, trying my best to navigate the safest path, despite the near complete darkness under the trees.

After a while my eyes start to adjust somewhat, and I know I'm heading in the right direction. There's not far to go now, but I need to cross a stream, and make my way up the opposite bank, and then navigate my way around the edge of the steep escarpment to approach from the lower side.

It would be treacherous in these conditions, I know, but I have little choice, and I start to descend the muddy bank towards the stream, which is swollen and flowing powerfully, fed by the intense rainwater running off from the surrounding high ground.

My horse approaches the river at an angle, plodding carefully over the mud at the edge of the river. I talk to her soothingly, trying to keep her calm. I let her stop to drink from the river for a moment, allowing us both a little time to rest.

Ted follows suit, lapping thirstily at the fast flowing water. I smile at my three-legged companion, suddenly glad that he'd decided to stay with me.

A bright flash of lightning startles all of us, and my horse lurches underneath me, bolting to the opposite bank, and charging up the muddy slope, struggling for purchase.

I try to calm her down, but my own panic only makes things worse. I pull hard on the reins in a final attempt to bring her to a halt, but it's a near fatal mistake. She resists the pull, turning sharply and rearing onto her hind legs for a moment.

When she lands, her front feet slip in the mud, and my heart jumps as she falls, whinnying in pain. I throw myself from her back, not wanting to get caught underneath her body, and land heavily on my side.

The air is punched from my lungs as I land, and for a horrible moment I can't breathe as the wind is knocked out of me. I struggle for air, but then finally manage to draw in a deep, ragged breath.

I glance over at the horse. She's lying on her side nearby, one of her forelegs held up protectively. My heart breaks at the sight; I dread to think what I'd have to do if she's broken her leg. There's just simply no way I could get her out of this ravine, even with Jett's help, and equally no way I could just leave her here to suffer.

I struggle to find purchase as I rise to my feet, only to slip again in the mud. My right ankle twists at a horrible angle, wrenching the joint and sending me back to the ground on my butt with a thump.

With a groan I start to crawl along the ground to reach my fallen horse, doing the only thing I can do now, rubbing her flanks gently in an attempt to keep her calm. I'm also soaked through, and glad for the warmth from her body.

I curse my stupidity and recklessness, closing my eyes shut tight to hold back more tears of anger and frustration. My eyes snap open at the sound of a deep, familiar voice, booming loud over the sound of the storm.

"Casey! Don't move, I'm coming to you!" Jett shouts, obviously having seen my plight.

I'm suddenly glad at his presence, even though I'm still pissed off at him.

I perch myself up on an elbow to peer out over the body of my horse to watch him approach, the bright light of a torch flashing over the ground in front of him as he picks his way towards us.

His horse remains calm; she's the older of the pair, and is rarely phased or startled. Flashes of lightning and booming thunder too little to distract her from plodding her careful and calm way towards us.

Jett climbs carefully from his horse and approaches, concern on his strong features. If the ride in the wind and rain has tired him, it doesn't show. He studies me, then the horse and then holds out a hand.

I reluctantly take his outstretched hand, and he pulls me firmly but gently to my feet.

"I'm sorry, Jett I just had to get out of there," I say.

He shakes his head dismissively.

"Don't worry about it. We'll talk when we've got you out of the rain," he says calmly. "What happened to your horse?"

"She panicked and slipped. I think it's her front right leg," I reply.

Jett kneels in front of the fallen horse, placing his hand on her snout and rubbing her gently, speaking in low, soothing tones. The horse seems mesmerized as he breathes the words into her nose, visibly calming.

I limp over to watch as he slowly takes the horse's injured leg into his strong hands, and gently probes the injured joint. All the while he's reassuring the horse, and my heart defrosts at the sight of him, working as if he'd never stopped being a vet.

He winces for a moment as the horse whinnies in pain as he flexes the joint, slowly at first, while pressing his palm on the horse's hoof. He winces again, and I suddenly fear the worst.

He glances up at me. And then smiles. I breathe a deep sigh of relief, and hobble over to his side.

CHAPTER ELEVEN

JETT

My initial worry that the horse had broken her ankle dissipates as I realize it's just a sprain. She'd obviously twisted it on the loose ground in her panic, and had been unable or unwilling to rise.

"It's not broken," I say to Casey, having to raise my voice above the wind howling through the trees at either side of the river bank. "But we need to get her on her feet, and get to shelter."

He looks down at me, and I notice he's hobbling, favoring his left leg.

"Can you walk?" I ask, studying him with concern.

He shrugs in response.

"Slowly!" he shouts back, smiling sheepishly.

Casey watches as I work, fashioning a makeshift splint for the horse from a length of sturdy wood, and tying it firmly above the ankle. With any luck, she should be able to walk off the sprain, or it would be a slow trek back to camp when the storm finally passes.

I tie her reins to the saddle of my horse, and gently push the older horse forward. The injured horse takes to her knees, and then shakily rises to her feet, encouraged by the presence of the old and calm mare.

With both animals now on their feet, I lead the front horse slowly up the bank, and to the sturdier ground within the woodland. With the horses out of the unstable ground, I head back to help Casey climb the bank to the trees.

I help him up into the saddle of the lead horse, and start to guide them through the trees, torch in hand as we pick our way carefully around the steep embankment next to us.

"There's some shelter down there," Casey says, pointing down to our right. "Should keep us out of the wind and the worst of the rain, at least."

The storm has hit fully now, and big droplets of rain are finding their way through the thick canopy above us. The wind howls through the forest, strong despite the shelter of the trees.

I lead the horses around the edge of the escarpment, and down towards the enclosed shelter. A familiar sight greets me, appearing from the trees. Casey's dog, trotting along happily, tongue lolling out, as if he's simply enjoying an afternoon stroll.

I shake my head and laugh at the sight, the dog's presence lifting my spirits a little.

As soon as we reach the bottom of the bank, the wind dies away, and the rain drops to a steady patter, no longer whipped into a painful frenzy by the gale. The trees open out into clearing as we reach the sheer face of the escarpment, providing us with a fairly dry sanctuary in the midst of the storm.

I help Casey down from the saddle, and we tend to the horses first. We brush them down and dry them as best as we can, before setting up a tarpaulin cover for them between some trees, and giving them some feed.

The tent follows next, pitched in the lee of the steep embankment. Then, finally, I fashion a makeshift shelter and bed for the dog, who settles down contentedly into the clothes I've laid down as bedding.

I turn to Casey, who's been putting on a tough face, despite the obvious pain he's in. He's shivering, too, and I know he's likely soaked through.

"You need to get in the tent and out of those clothes," I say.

A flash of angry defiance crosses his features, before his shoulders slump in defeat and he makes his slow way over and into the tent.

He still hasn't forgiven me, despite my rescue. Can't say that I blame him, though. I guess I've got some explaining to do.

I give him a few minutes, grabbing the cooking supplies, some clean clothes and a towel, before opening the flap of the large tent and heading inside.

Casey's at the back of the tent, still shivering as he sits in a sleeping bag, only his head poking from it.

"Are you going to explain what was in that folder, Jett?" he asks. "And it better be good or whatever we have, whatever... *this* is, is over."

I nod as I remove my outer layer of wet clothes and place them at the foot of the tent, and start to set up the covered stove. For warmth, and to prepare some food.

"What you saw was true, Casey. It happened, all of it. And I still feel terrible about it to this day," I say with regret.

He frowns at me.

"So you say. But how... *why* did you let it happen? Are you trying to tell me that you're some kind of reformed monster? How am I supposed to believe that?" he replies, voice trembling with anger.

"We didn't. Not directly, at least. It all started when the business picked up. Those of us that founded the company, we set aside our day jobs, and sold the veterinarian practice. What became a side project took over our lives quite quickly, and before long most of us stepped away from the demands of the company, as it skyrocketed overnight.

"We were lucky. Right products, medicinal and cosmetic, selling them for the right price, at the right time."

Casey shuffles over to approach the heat of the burner, studying me with interest as I tell the story.

"I ended up falling into the role of CEO. No one else wanted it. We were ex-vets, no one else really had a business brain or was willing to make the hard decisions. But I loved it, it drove me. I became obsessed with growing the business, watching it thrive.

"We had more orders than we could fill. Our clients were getting pissed as we delayed orders, and we struggled to develop new products with the strain on the company."

I sigh, and shake my head at the naiveté I'd shown in my desperation to save the company from failure.

"So, that's where Mosner Corp came in. They approached me, out of the blue. Said they could help with product development, testing and production.

They would do it quicker and for less than our current contractors, and they had the capacity we needed.

I pause to place a pan on the stove, and glance at Casey.

"When something sounds too good to be true," he says ruefully. "It usually is."

I grunt in agreement.

"Yeah. I wish I could go back in time and tell myself that. Maybe with a slap or two around the head. Anyway, I made the decision to take them on. Business boomed overnight. We were filling orders within weeks, churning out the products at an incredible rate, undercutting the competition and retaining a healthy profit margin.

"I thought I'd made it as the money started pouring it. I thought that was it, that I'd found success and could walk away. All of us, the original shareholders, soon became millionaires. The lucky ones, those that had taken a back seat or walked away, but retained considerable shares in the company, didn't have to deal with the fallout that was to follow."

"The animal testing," Casey adds.

"You got it," I respond. "None of us knew the corners Mosner Corp were cutting. Their business model was based on being bigger and more efficient than their competitors, and it all added up. On paper, at least. So we left them to do their thing, and just fronted the company, building the client base up.

"Then, one day, there was an exposé from an environmental activist group. Mosner was using dated and illegal testing methods in their labs under tight security, but the group infiltrated the company. It was ordered to close its labs, and effectively closed down overnight. And then attention turned to us."

Casey's expression softens.

"So what did you do?" he asks quietly.

I shrug.

"The only thing I could do, like I'm doing now. Tell the truth. We went public, admitting our mistake, and vowing to reform our company. We were hit with a hefty fine, to be paid out to various charities and foundations of the district attorney's choosing.

"We almost went bankrupt, and share prices plummeted. But we held to our promise, funded the projects and paid the fine in full. And I brought the business back from the brink, making personally sure that nothing like it ever happened again."

I take a breath, relieved that I'd had the opportunity to explain myself. Now it was down to Casey to decide if I've truly changed.

"Hold on," he says. "You paid the debt in full? But why... I mean, the continued funding? Couldn't you have stopped?"

I shrug.

"Like I said before, I care. I saw the great work our money was doing, and I didn't want to pull the plug. I set up a foundation, funneling a portion of our profits, and regular payments from my personal fortune to the charity. And I've never looked back. It was guilt that drove me initially, but now... well, I guess I'd say it's passion."

"Thanks for telling me the truth," he says. "But I need some time to think this all over. What's happened in the last few days, well, it's all been a bit much."

I smile warmly at him.

"Let's eat, and get some rest. Sleep on it. We can talk tomorrow, if you're ready."

I set about preparing dinner as Casey settles down next to me, seeming content and looking much warmer, his eyes half closed and glazed with exhaustion.

CHAPTER TWELVE

CASEY

I wake up with a start, slowly realizing that I'd immediately fallen into a deep, restful sleep after eating, and after Jett had taken a look at my ankle and given me some painkillers.

Luckily it was just sprained, he said, but I'd need an x-ray to be sure there's no fractures, and I'd need to rest it for a few weeks, at least.

I'm a little angry with myself about the way I'd acted, how my fears of letting someone in had taken over so strongly, and caused me to act so rashly. But I was glad Jett had told me the truth, and I could see the anguish and regret in his eyes as he'd told me the story.

He obviously still carried a weight of guilt on his broad shoulders, but I knew that wasn't the only thing that drove him. He truly cared, and the man I'd got to know over the first few days we'd been together was the real Jett. Handsome, kind, gentle yet strong and confident.

I suddenly realize that I've very quickly grown used to his company, his reassuring presence by my side, and mixed emotions course through me as it dawns on me that he could disappear forever, even tomorrow, if there was a break in the storm.

I place my hand on his shoulder and shake him awake gently, wanting to hear his voice, to have his eyes fixed on mine.

He wakes with a start, turning over in his separate sleeping bag to study me with concern.

"Casey? Are you OK?" he asks.

I feel dumb as my emotions get the better of me, and I feel a tear threaten to run down my cheek.

"Jett I... just promise me you won't leave me. Okay?" I say, the words tumbling out without thought.

I redden in embarrassment at the admission of my feelings for him, suddenly nervous that maybe he doesn't feel the same way.

He caresses my cheek with a large hand, wiping away the single tear. His expression is soft and gentle.

"I promise. I don't want to leave you, Casey. I've fallen for you. Hard. And I want you," he replies in a soft whisper.

I'm still naked underneath my sleeping bag, and I feel a thrill of sexual desire, the frustration strengthened by the stresses of the day. I want to feel Jett close to me, inside me, and forget about everything else.

I slowly unzip the side of my sleeping bag, exposing my naked body. Jett's eyes widen at the sight of my erection and his breathing increases, and I watch him study my body in the dim, early morning light seeping through the walls of the tent.

"Come here," I growl suggestively. "Show me how *hard* you've fallen for me."

He unzips his own sleeping bag eagerly, and slides out of it and into mine. He's only wearing boxer shorts, and his arousal is obvious even in the dim light.

He lies himself on top of me, his swelling erection brushing against the sensitive skin of my own, and I feel a tingle of pleasure run through me.

I hold his body tight against mine as we kiss. His tongue entering my mouth to caress mine. Jett's breath is hot against me as we kiss passionately, his clean scent turning me on even more as he fills my senses.

I gasp as he lowers his face to kiss at my neck, working his way down to my chest, where he stops for a moment to take a sensitive nipple into his mouth. He opens his mouth wide as he sucks at me hard, tracing his tongue in circles around the peak of my nipple.

He throws open the sleeping bag as he makes his way further down my body, his lips and tongue caressing the skin of my stomach. He positions himself between my legs, being gentle with my ankle and pushing it to one side with a firm hand on my inner thigh.

I feel my rock hard cock bob in anticipation, and I'm already hot and swollen in anticipation of his touch. My breathing is heavy as I watch him run his tongue around my balls, kissing along my inner thigh.

I gasp as he suddenly takes the head of my cock between his lips, teasing the ridge of my glans, sucking on me, his tongue darting fast in circles around my head.

His stubble scratches the inside of my thighs as he pushes my cock into his throat, and I shudder with pleasure as his tongue works its way up and down my shaft. I move my hips involuntarily with the movement of his tongue, squirming and moaning as he pleasures me.

I grasp the back of Jett's head, pressing myself as deep into his throat as he can take me, and close my eyes, losing myself in the moment as waves of almost painful pleasure shoot through me. He speeds up the movements of his tongue, and I let out a soft yelp as he suddenly grasps my balls with one of his strong hands.

I twitch and shudder against him, grinding my swollen rock hard cock into his face. He senses that I'm about to orgasm, and stops suddenly. I gasp with frustration as he rises to his knees, his face flushed red and wet with his own saliva.

"Not yet," he says hoarsely.

Jett swivels his hips and twists himself around so he's facing away from me. He presents himself to me, bending over to rest on his elbows and knees, his hips angled up in the air, tempting me to enter him.

Jett looks over his shoulder at me, to see me pull down his boxer shorts. Now his cock swings free, bobbing erect below his stomach as it's released from the confines of his underwear.

"Fuck me, Casey," he says, not wanting me to tease him anymore. "Fuck me hard."

He watches as I approach him, shuffling forward on my knees, my thick cock held in my hand. He places both of his hands on the cheeks of his ass and watches as I guide myself into him.

I gasp out loud as he pushes himself back onto my cock, and I enter him much more quickly than I had planned, stretching him around my thick girth. Our eyes meet, and there's a look on his face, of frustration and desperation.

I pant and nod at him in encouragement.

"Yes, that's it," I gasp. "You want it."

He reaches behind to claw at my legs with both hands now, pulling me tight as he pushes his ass onto the full length of my hard shaft. I feel his butt slap against my stomach as I'm fully engorged by him.

Jett slides himself up and down my length, in and out of him over and over again, and I howl as he thrusts back into me, deep and hard. He repeats the movement, slowly pulling forward, and then thrusting back into me.

His cock bounces each time he thrusts himself back into me, and I push my torso up so I'm resting on my hands on his hips, allowing my cock as deep into him as it will go.

My hands begin to grasp his waist and hips tightly, using them for purchase as I begin to fuck him harder and harder, increasing in pace. He responds by thrusting back harder, faster, grunting with pleasure and breathing heavily at the exertion.

Frustration and pleasure mingle and become one as my body slaps repeatedly against his, my thick cock stretching him to his very limit with each thrust.

I gasp and shudder, the orgasm I'd start to feel building returning strongly, making my knees shake. I lift my head and loud out a howl of pleasure as I start to climax.

The orgasm is powerful, sending shockwaves of painful pleasure to my very core, my cock throbbing incredibly hard, muscles twitching at the release of sexual tension.

"Oh, fuck," Jett says breathlessly.

He gasps, almost as if in pain, and I feel my cum shoot deep into him as he yells back in pleasure, his body shuddering against mine. I still fuck him hard as he clenches around me and cums, and he sags forward as his energy fades, slowly being replaced by a warm afterglow.

I thrust into Jett one final time, and then slow, gasping for air, my hands gripping his hips tight as I reach the peak of my orgasm.

I feel my body sag forwards against his, and I'm suddenly spent.

"Wow," he gasps as I slip out of him. "That sure was something."

I manage a grunt of approval.

"Yeah. It sure was. After that apology, I think you're forgiven," I say, with a contented smile on my face.

The next morning we rise early, and make our slow, and for me and the injured horse, slightly painful way back to the ranger cabin.

The cabin has survived the storm without any damage, to our relief, and Jett sets up the radio antenna so we can call in to headquarters.

I reluctantly admit what had happened over the radio, deciding to leave out the part about my angry flight, saying instead that we'd got caught out during an excursion after the first storm had passed.

Luckily, there's a ranger on standby to fill in for me while I recover, and now that the worst of the storms have passed, they can send the ranger along with a vet, via helicopter, and take Jett and I away to the city.

I thank the radio operator, and sign out before turning off the radio. Jett takes my hand in his, and pulls me to my feet gently.

He takes me in an embrace, burying my face into his muscular neck.

"The helicopter will be here in a few hours," I say, my voice muffled.

"Right. Now, you need to rest," he replies.

He tosses my arm around his shoulders and helps me to the couch, where he sets me down. He lifts my injured leg, placing my ankle on the armrest to elevate my foot.

"Thank you," I say, holding one of his hands in both of mine. "For everything."

He smiles down at me.

"It should be me thanking you," he replies.

I frown at his words.

"Thanking me for what?" I ask.

His expression softens with emotion, and he leans down to give me a kiss.

"For reminding me who I really am," he whispers, before kissing me again.

EPILOGUE

JETT

"**W**ell I for one think I echo the rest of us here when I say, Jett, that I'm glad you decided to step aside from the company's board," one of the non-executive directors on the charity foundation's board says.

The board meeting is coming to a close. It's the first meeting I've attended since finally managing to step aside from the day to day role of CEO, after a long five months of first finding and then handing my responsibilities over to a suitable replacement.

I hold my hands up, and smile warmly.

"I'm not fully out of it yet, unfortunately," I respond with a hint of regret. "I'm still taking on an advisory role for the next few months, and helping out when needed. But I'll have much more time to work with you all, which I'm greatly looking forward to."

There's a general murmur of approval around the table, and all eyes are on me for a moment.

"Have we all had a chance to review the proposed funding of the Taylor initiative?" I ask the room.

Mike Lincoln, who has decided to join me on the board, nods in assent.

"Yes. The information was disseminated. Looks like an excellent initiative to me, building on the great work we've started out in the reserve. Mustang herds are thriving, and the environment is flourishing, by all accounts. All in favor of approval of full-funding?" he says.

The vote passes in unanimous approval, and there's a spring in my step as I leave the room, with today's business concluded.

I decide to surprise Casey at work. He's taken up a role in our research and development labs, after accepting a scholarship to study as a veterinarian, which he's doing alongside his research work.

I'd initially offered to pay for him to train, but being proud and stubborn, he'd refused. He wanted to work for his training. So, I'd called in a few favors and got him a scholarship, with the plan of having him as a resident veterinarian on one of our new reserves at some point in the future.

And, he didn't know it yet, but I was planning on joining him. Just me and Casey, in our own cabin, out in a reserve we could call our own, doing what we both cared for the most.

The lab is in one of the basement levels of the high rise office building I'm in, and I'm strangely nervous as the lift descends, seemingly taking an age to travel from the top of the building down to near the bottom.

The door pings and slides open, and I steel myself with a breath as I head out into the lab, heading for Casey's office.

His office is empty, and I head into the lab. A few faces look up at me, then return to their work. It's not uncommon for me to wander in on occasion, usually when I was missing Casey and wanted to share a few moments with him.

"He's in the next room," a lab assistant says with a smile, pointing to a door next to her.

I walk through to find Casey piping a liquid into a few test tubes, deep concentration on his face as he works.

He doesn't notice me for a moment, then looks up. A broad smile spreads across his handsome features, making my heart skip a beat.

"Good news," I say.

His eyes widen in surprise and he combs his fingers through his hair in nervous anticipation.

"They approved the funding," I continue. "We can get started on - oof!"

My words are cut short as he flies into my arms, and I laugh as I take him into an embrace, squeezing him with all of my strength.

"So when you've finished training, we can get out there. Make a real difference," I say, and kiss him on the tip of his nose.

He leans back in my arms, eyes meeting mine.

"We?" he asks.

"Yes, we. I promised I wouldn't leave you, didn't I? And I always keep my promises."

I feel nerves in the pit of my stomach, and reach a hand into my pants pocket.

"Which kind of leads on to this," I say, and step back.

He roars in delight as I drop to one knee, and take the jewelry box from my pocket and open it. A shiny pair of tungsten bands glean up at me, each framing a single mahogany colored band of fossilized bone, both set into an elegant, velvet ring case.

I turn the box to face him.

"Will you marry me?" I ask.

He's silent for a moment, his usually red face white with shock. His mouth opens for a moment, and then closes again.

"I... yes, Jett! Of course I will!" he says, and guides me to my feet to plant a big kiss on my lips.

I place the ring on his left ring finger, he situates mine for me, and we embrace again.

"Actually, this is probably a good time to talk to you about the future," he says. "I've been thinking about a few things."

I raise an eyebrow, and study Casey. His eyes sparkle as he keeps the suspense for a moment, a small, slightly nervous grin on his full lips.

He leans in to me, and his lips brush against my ear.

"I've been thinking... I really want a family," he whispers.

I'm frozen in shock at his words, and it's suddenly my turn to be left speechless. He frowns at me in concern, and taps me lightly on the chest.

"Kids. I don't know if it's through adoption or surrogacy, or how it's going to happen but I need to be a father."

His voice trails off, and shock is slowly replaced by excitement at the prospect of this new adventure. I try to lift Casey from his feet, but he's just a little too heavy for me so it turns into another bear hug. He growls in delight, and all eyes are on us as we practically float through the lab, into his office, so we can celebrate more intimately.

EPILOGUE

CASEY

I leave the main road and head out into our newly established reserve, driving along a worn, dusty track in my truck towards the ranger station. The reserve isn't quite as big as the one I'd looked after previously, and is on the very edge of the wild prairies, meaning we are not so remote and a little closer to civilization.

The drive to the cabin still takes a while, but I feel at peace, enjoying the scenery as it passes me by, and I drum my fingers on the wheel to the music playing quietly through the truck's stereo.

I finally reach our new home, and the scale of the recently built cabin still takes my breath away as I approach it.

Jett and I had it custom made, built with a traditional timber frame but with plenty of modern touches, and much larger in scale than the usual, functional ranger station cabins.

Well, it is our family home, after all. And Jett had insisted no expense was spared to make the place as comfortable and modern as possible. We even had a gym built, complete with sauna, Jacuzzi and steam room, with a small swimming pool. There were plenty of bedrooms, a dining room and large kitchen, a games room for the kids, and even a guest suite.

The place is huge. But we both love it.

I smile warmly at the sight of our two kids playing with Ted out in the yard. The dog is old now and as scruffy as ever, but was still tireless, and loved playing with our adopted son and daughter, Jake and Theresa.

I park up, the noise of the truck drawing the attention of my kids and my three legged companion. All three rush over to me, acting as if they haven't seen me for days.

"Daddy!" Theresa calls, the toddler stumbling behind her older brother as she runs awkwardly towards me.

I laugh at the welcome, and my heart warms at the sight of my kids. I take them up into my arms, and squeeze them in a tight embrace.

"I hope you were good for Papa while Daddy was working," I say through a smile.

Jake frowns at me, as if I've just asked the most stupid question in the world.

"We're always good. Aren't we, 'Resa?" he says seriously.

She giggles at her brother.

"We are always *very* good. Did you save the animals?" she asks, her little face contorted with concern.

I carry the kids towards the cabin, wondering how long it will be until they're too heavy to pick up.

"Yes, Daddy saved them. They were just a little bit sick and needed some medicine, that's all," I reply as I walk through into the cabin, and set the kids down on the polished wooden floor.

They rush off in separate directions, off to cause mayhem, no doubt.

I walk through the house to find my husband. He's in his office, and I can hear him talking at his computer as I gently tap on the door and walk in.

He waves at me as I enter, and I smile back at him. I watch him as he talks, evidently in the middle of a tele-conference or video meeting.

We'd had a satellite system set up to bring high speed internet to the cabin, allowing for Jett to be based out here, and still take part in board meetings and discussions. The rest of the time we spent out in the reserve together, or on the road as visiting veterinarians for the surrounding farms and small towns.

He's engrossed in the conversation, and I take the opportunity to study his muscular frame, clearly visible beneath the tight t shirt he's wearing. He raises an eyebrow at me, and I give him a cheeky wink.

Jett holds up a finger, and blows me a kiss. Before long he's thanking everyone, and then switches the computer screen off.

"Hey, babe," he says, rising to his feet. "Board wanted an update on the project. I told them it's going great. I mean, what did they expect with us as the ranger team?"

"How did it go over at the Hudson farm?" he asks.

I shrug nonchalantly.

"No big deal. Just a few animals a bit under the weather. A course of antibiotics should do the trick, and I've told them to get in touch if they worsen," I respond.

He walks over to me and takes me into his arms, studying my features.

"Did you hear the weather report? Storms are due tonight. Heavy storms, for a few days," he says.

Jett wraps me up in his arms, and pulls my body against his.

"I was thinking we could... re-enact our first few days together. What do you think?" he asks, his voice low.

I kiss him on the lips, and lean to whisper in his ear.

"Sounds good, cowboy. Let's see if you've still got it."

We kiss again, eliciting a shout from a spying child.

"Ewww!" Jake shouts. "'Resa, Daddy and Papa are kissing!"

My eyes lock with Jett's, and we both burst out laughing, both completely oblivious to the fact that we had an audience.

"When the kids are in bed, I'm gonna take you up on that," I say quietly.

Jett sets me free, and turns to his son. He raises his arms and lets out an animal roar, and Jake squeals with delight as his fathers chase him out into the cabin.

Be the first to find out about all of Dillon Hart's new releases, book sales, and freebies by joining his VIP Mailing List. Join today and get a FREE book -- instantly! Join by clicking here!

ABOUT THE AUTHOR

Dillon Hart, who lives in San Francisco, writes compelling gay romance novels that embody the essence of love and human relationships. His works are inspired by the diverse communities that call the city home, from the vibrant Castro neighborhood to the bohemian Mission district. In his spare time, Dillon enjoys riding the F Line streetcar from Market Street to Fisherman's Wharf, where he enjoys the ocean breezes and the bustle of the waterfront.

More on www.dillonhart.com

Join my newsletter by clicking here.

Write me at contact@dillonhart.com

FIND ME ON SOCIAL MEDIA